Praise for
THE RETRIEVAL ARTIST SERIES

One of the top ten greatest science fiction detectives of all time.

—io9

[Miles Flint is] one of 14 great sci-fi and fantasy detectives who out-Sherlock'd Holmes. [Flint] is a candidate for the title of greatest fictional detective of all time.

—Blastr

What links [Miles Flint] to his most memorable literary ancestors is his hard-won ability to perceive the complex nature of morality and live with the burden of his own inevitable failure.

—Locus

The SF thriller is alive and well, and today's leading practitioner is Kristine Kathryn Rusch.

—Analog

Also by
Kristine Kathryn Rusch

Alien Influences
Snipers
The End of The World (novella)
The Retrieval Artist Series

The Diving Universe:

NOVELLAS

Diving into the Wreck
The Room of Lost Souls
Becalmed
Becoming One with the Ghosts
Stealth
Strangers at the Room of Lost Souls
The Spires of Denon

NOVELS

Diving into the Wreck
City of Ruins
Boneyards
Skirmishes

Praise for
KRISTINE KATHRYN RUSCH

Kristine Kathryn Rusch is one of the best writers in the field.

—SFRevu

[Retrieval Artist Miles Flint is] one of the top ten greatest science fiction detectives of all time.

—io9

The SF thriller is alive and well, and today's leading practitioner is Kristine Kathryn Rusch.

—Analog

A well-conceived, well-executed novel.

—The New York Times Book Review
on *Alien Influences*

…a fast paced whodunit …*Snipers* is an excellent amalgamation of history, thriller, mystery & science fiction.

—Dave Dickinson, Astroguyz, on *Snipers*

Chilling murders, mind-blowing suspense, a touch of time travel and a bit of romance combine to a thought-provoking, entertaining vacation from reality.

—RT Book Reviews on *Snipers*

Praise for
DIVING INTO THE WRECK

Rusch delivers a page-turning space adventure while contemplating the ethics of scientists and governments working together on future tech.

—Publisher's Weekly

This is classic sci-fi, a well-told tale of dangerous exploration. The first-person narration makes the reader an eyewitness to the vast, silent realms of deep space, where even the smallest error will bring disaster. Compellingly human and technically absorbing, the suspense builds to fevered intensity, culminating in an explosive yet plausible conclusion.

—RT Book Reviews Top Pick

Rusch's handling of the mystery and adventure is stellar, and the whole tale proves quite entertaining.

—Booklist Online

The technicalities in Boss' story are beautifully played…. She's real, flawed, and interesting…. Read the book. It is very good.

—SFFWorld.com

WINDCHIMES

KRISTINE KATHRYN RUSCH

*wmg*PUBLISHING

Broken Windchimes

Published 2013 by WMG Publishing
www.wmgpublishing.com
First published in *Asimov's SF Magazine*, September, 2009
Cover art copyright © Rolffimages/Dreamstime
Book and cover design copyright © 2013
by WMG Publishing
Cover design by
Allyson Longueira/WMG Publishing
ISBN-13: 978-0-615-84895-2
ISBN-10: 0-615-84895-8

BROKEN
WINDCHIMES

1

I FIRST HEARD NON-PANÉ MUSIC in an alley behind an auditorium in Lhelomika. Lhelomika, the arts capitol of Djapé, made me nervous. The last two times I had performed there, I shivered as I hit each note—not with cold, but with fear.

That afternoon, I walked outside the auditorium, trying to calm myself. From a nearby building, I heard a raspy male voice—a deep unaltered adult male voice—attempting to sing a melody. Some instruments I could not identify provided a music bed behind the voice.

The instruments were more harmonious than the voice, even though they did not hit pure tones. But the voice held me. It sang of a wonderful world, one that had beauty in its simple existence.

Strangely, the harshness of the voice, its lack of tone and musicality, provided a contrast to the lyrics so profound that it accented them.

I stood outside the building, listening as the song played, knowing that this was human music and it was forbidden to me. If Gibson, my manager, caught me, he would chastise me. Male sopranos who performed as long as I had—some twenty years now—were rare, a commodity worth millions.

Each day that I survived in my rarified position as performer—a living windchime, as the Pané called us—was a victory. I knew my time was limited.

Maybe that was why, when I made it through that evening's performance with no mistakes, I hid in my study and searched for that song on the forbidden human databases.

I didn't find it for months.

When I did, I listened, rapt, as stunned as I had been the first time at the simple beauty of contrast, the way that the flaws added to the whole.

The Pané would never accept flaws.

I knew it, and ignored it.

And some would argue, that was the beginning of the end.

2

I SANG MY LAST CONCERT before a packed hall in Tygher City. The auditorium there, made of bone and thin membranes almost like skin, had acoustics so perfect that a sigh made on stage could be heard in each seat, in every row. Only the best performers got a berth in Tygher City, and I'd played there for fifteen of my twenty-five summers.

On this evening, I sang three solos accompanied by the Boys' Choir, all in the second half of the concert, and all written by Tampini.

Tampini composed for male windchimes, accenting their technique and vocal range. His work, very Pané, was rarely performed outside of the Tygher City auditorium, since it was one of the few places on Djapé that had the acoustic sensitivity for his works.

The auditorium in Tygher City made me nervous. A note, missed by as little as one-one-thousandth, would receive silence, the Pané version of a boo. Even timing that did not follow the score to the letter—say, a half note extended to a dotted half simply for interpretation—had gotten more than one performer thrown off the stage.

So I had dreaded the performance for weeks, and shaved my involvement from six solos to three. Even then, I couldn't lose the feeling of impending doom.

I had mentioned that to Gibson, and he had laughed at me, telling me I worried too much. Still, he had the on-site doctor take my temperature and give me a thorough going over to make certain there were no alien viruses coursing through my system. They couldn't give me any medication to keep my blood pressure steady because medication might make an alteration, even a slight one, in my vocal chords. Nor could they feed me to keep my blood sugar up, because food coated the throat, disturbed the stomach, and occasionally caused gas.

More than one performer had lost his berth in Tygher City because of a nearly silent swallowed belch.

All that preparation, all the careful rehearsal—my time monitored so that I didn't overdo—, and still I approached the edge of the shell-like stage with trepidation.

It didn't show, of course. I walked on stage with a fake confidence born of years of performing. I wore a blue robe that contrasted with the chorus's white, and reflected the natural interior light of the bone auditorium as if we were outdoors.

The Pané crowded in their seats, squat and attentive, their heads down so that they could hear better. They were oddly malleable creatures, mostly cartilage, their skin a translucent gray that showed the shadows of their internal organs.

Their faces, it was said, took a lot of getting used to: eyes askew, mouth hidden, and the ridges that looked like sheet wrinkles, covering the bulk of their skull. The Pané looked normal to me, but I really couldn't remember the times before I arrived on Djapé. Like so many of my companions, my voice came early. Someone discovered my hollow, fluted soprano before I had turned three.

The first part of the set went well. The boys' choir had a sweetness that the adult male sopranos lost. Or perhaps it was the innocence in their faces, the love of singing that also got lost after years of performing.

The children took on Tampini like he was meant to be sung, with precision and grace and harmonies that sent shivers up my spine. The Pané remained motionless, so attentive that they barely seemed to breathe. I sang the first solo, the hardest of the three, with a clarity of tone that I hadn't realized I could achieve.

The problems started in the second solo which was, really, more of a descant. I felt a thickness at the back of my throat, as if phlegm were creeping in. I had the desperate urge to cough, but consummate performer that I was, I did not. Coughing ruined the vocal chords and had to be avoided at all costs. Clearing the throat and shouting had the same effect, and I hadn't done any of those things in my memory.

But I wanted to, right there on stage, in front of five thousand rapt Pané.

When the second Tampini ended, and I was allowed to walk backstage before taking my second bow, I swigged the warm water Gibson kept for me. It cleared the throat slightly, refreshed me enough, and got rid of the urge to cough.

In fact, I had forgotten all about it as I started into the third solo.

This last, a Pané favorite, always seemed the least musical to me. The boys provided a choral backdrop, usually made up of thirds and fifths, while I let my four-octave voice explore its range. At the time, I was the only man on Djapé who could hit the E above High C, and Gibson exploited that as often as he could, having me sing show-off pieces like Tampini's Aria in E Major.

The aria had an optional arpeggio section, and Gibson always made me include it at Tygher City. To the human ear, the arpeggios sounded like little more than exercises, going from E major to Bb minor, and on through every possible variation, until the mind wearied and human listener grew bored.

But the Pané heard overtones and undertones we could not. A series of arpeggios like that apparently created harmonies that lingered, pleasing the Pané like no other musical trick could. Any performer who could do the Aria in E Major and do it well was a guaranteed celebrity on Djapé.

The aria had become my signature piece, much as I despised it.

I was right in the middle of the C Major arpeggio when my voice cracked.

It didn't break the way voices do when they change—I'd heard that a few times, and it was a horrible thing, especially the look on the boy's face when he realized his treatment was faulty, and the thing that he had lived his entire life for, the thing that defined him, was vanishing.

No. Instead, my voice cracked with exhaustion, leaving a hole between the G's. Even though I found High C, felt it position properly in my vocal chords, the note did not emerge. Instead, there was a wisp of air, a near-silence, almost a hiss that was audible throughout that galaxy's most sensitive auditorium.

The audience gasped. It was a hideous, non-human sound. The Pané attempted to imitate us, out of a sense of courtesy, but it backfired. Their gasp was closer to a roar, emerging from the throat and not the diaphragm.

It was a sharp, shocked sound, one in such a low register that the Pané couldn't hear it.

But I could, and it terrified me. They had made the sound in my presence maybe a hundred times before, but never once directed at me.

Still, my training paid off. I did not lose my place or my concentration, and when High C was part of an arpeggio again, I hit the note with the same clarity and purity that I had always had.

I finished the piece and walked off the stage to lukewarm applause, knowing that my career was finished.

Gibson, to his credit, tried to smooth the moment over as if it hadn't mattered at all. His puffy face looked pasty in the backstage lights, and his hair seemed even thinner than before.

He put his fleshy hands on my back, easing me toward the dressing room.

"No need to worry," he said. "We'll get it checked out. You just should have told me."

Told him what? My voice had never broken, never failed me, not even when I'd gone on stage with fevers, and mysterious Pané-originated illnesses.

I had never failed before—not in twenty-two years.

I had no idea how to react.

Neither did anyone else.

3

I RECEIVED THREE DAYS OF TESTING, all in the port city of Énané, as far from the Pané music scene as we could get. Énané was the site of the largest human enclave on Djapé, and as such, a place that most Pané escaped as soon as they could.

The Pané found most humans large, smelly, and loud; we had been of no use to them at all until they discovered our musical abilities, centuries ago. At first the Pané thought the abilities mindless, simple pleasant sounds that we made almost unconsciously. Over time, however, the Pané realized that we purposely made music, that we had control over the notes, the order in which they were sung or played, and the interpretation of those notes.

Still, it took time for the Pané to understand what we were doing—and time for us to understand the Pané. Their highly evolved hearing found pleasure only in the diatonic scale, and then mostly in notes above Middle C.

Certain instruments—the organ, for example, and the harpsichord—caused the Pané pain when played in that register. Flutes, clarinets, oboes could be tolerated, but brass instruments could not. Stringed instruments, particularly the violin, were banned on Djapé. While humans heard the violin as an expressive instrument, imitative of the human voice, the Pané heard it only as a scraping of bow on string, a grating sound that was so repulsive to them that, legend has it, the first Pané who ever heard one murdered the violinist.

Human music had strict limits, and had to remain in the human enclave. Until the Pané discovered the soprano—the male soprano.

And Pané were particular about their male sopranos. Falsettos, tried once and quickly abandoned, were almost as offensive as a violin. Irish tenors fell into the same category. The male soprano had to have had a clear voice from boyhood, and that voice couldn't be tainted by anything that would offend the sensitive Pané ear.

No human ever learned if the Pané were truly as sensitive as they claimed or if they were, like all true collectors, so fussy that they couldn't stand the idea of tampering with a pure voice. For the Pané were collectors of the worst sort.

They could not create music of their own. Their vocal chords did not produce song and they could not envision music. Djapé itself had many musical aspects—from the ice caves of Windsor to the Trilling Beetles of Lahonia—but nothing formal, nothing creatively musical.

The Pané didn't know that music could be created purposely until the first humans arrived on Djapé, centuries ago. I never learned how the alliance between the Pané and the humans was formed, nor did I know, then, how it was maintained.

No one answered those questions, often pretending they didn't hear them. Instead, I got to study music management and practice my scales.

The older I got, the less any of that appealed to me, and I could tell no one. By that point, I was Djapé's biggest human star: a favorite windchime who could perform in the most difficult venues at the best hours.

All of that ended for me with a single missed note, a crack, a lost C, scarcely noticeable to human ears, and serious flaw to the Pané.

I had enjoyed my success, and while I had always known that I would one day cease being the biggest star, I had hoped to remain respected—the kind of performer called out for a nostalgic review or, if my voice had suffered the effects of age, a commentary on past performances, often done before an audience.

I had even imagined my retirement—on the rugged coastline between Énané and the Causée Mountain— where I would teach advanced students (only those who had the capability of becoming stars) and where I would occasionally deign to review an up-and-coming performer, give someone a small lift, like I had gotten early on, enabling him to become a performer the Pané might worship.

None of that was possible now. I knew it, and my assistants knew it. One afternoon, I caught Gibson leaving the compound in the company of a boy. The boy, at that indeterminate age between twelve and twenty, had a softness that belonged only to the human musicians on Djapé. When he saw me, he flushed.

If I had needed confirmation of the severity of my situation, I had it then. Gibson—who only handled the best—was looking for a new client. As soon as he found the boy he could develop into a star, Gibson would be gone.

I fled to the garden, pushing my way past the leafy foliage until I found my favorite stone bench. It was tucked into a side corner, not tended often, because the small lemon and orange trees didn't need as much day-to-day care. I huddled on the bench, put my hands behind me, and turned my face to Djapé's hot sun. I wasn't supposed to do that either—something about the light and my skin—but I didn't have to listen to Gibson any more.

He was leaving.

And I was shaking.

I had never before been on my own.

4

HE CAUGHT ME, hours later, in the study, listening to the song I had heard in the alley so long ago. I had found it, startled at its age. The singer was a 20th century American composer, and trumpeter named Louis Armstrong. Until that evening, I'd always listened to Armstrong on headphones, secretly, hiding him. He was a revelation in surround sound—a gravelly voice that would make the Pané recoil in fear.

Gibson acted as if he were still my manager, as if he were not going to leave me at all. "What's this?"

I hadn't heard him come in. I had been lost in the archaic slang of the Armstrong.

My back had been to Gibson, but I did not whirl to face him as I would have done just the day before. Instead, I waited until the end of the phrase, then touched the sound file built into my desk. The music paused mid-note.

"Is that what destroyed your voice? That garbage?" Gibson had apparently continued speaking over the music, and I hadn't noticed. Now that the music was off, his voice was much too loud.

I turned, as I would toward a fan, folding my hands together over my robe.

"Have you noticed," I asked, keeping my voice at its usual whisper, "that we listen to very little music in this house?"

"Pané-inspired music is not restful to human ears," Gibson snapped. "When you are not performing or practicing, you need to relax."

He had said that a thousand times, maybe more. I nodded. "How is the new client?"

Gibson's eyes narrowed. I had never spoken to him like that before. "It was a lunch."

"It was an audition," I said. "We've been together for twenty-two years. You owe me the courtesy of honesty."

He glanced at the sound file and I knew what he was going to say. He was going to make this about me, about my words, about my problems. *Did you imitate this so-called singer? What were you thinking?*

In the past, I would have answered him humbly. I would have let him take my music away.

He turned away from me, but not before I saw guilt cross his face. He sank into the couch and put his feet on the ottoman. He seemed relaxed, but he was not. The fingers of his left hand drummed against the multi-lined Pané-made upholstery.

"I only move up," he said. "The moment I start the spiral downward, even with a client I care about, I lose my clout."

I crossed my arms, hiding my clenched fists beneath my biceps. Spiral downward. Loss of clout.

Loss of everything.

Not only would I lose my career and my dreamed-of future, I also would lose the only family I had ever known.

Perhaps, deep down, I had felt that I could hold him here, with guilt, with logic, with sheer affection.

Even with a client I care about. Client. Care. Not friend. Not love.

He had held himself distant from me, even when I was a three-year-old prodigy with a spectacular voice. Even then he had evaluated my every note, my every performance, and if he hadn't felt I was on an upward path, he would have left.

I was shaking, but I tried to control it. I did not want him to see the effect his words were having on me.

"You have enough money, you know that. You don't have to work again, if you don't want to. That's why I taught you how to handle and understand finances. That's more than most managers would have done for you."

He sounded defensive. He *was* defensive. But he was also right. He had forced me to study things I had not wanted to learn. Money, business, even booking schedules.

Teaching me how to survive the inevitable decline. Always with an eye toward the next client, the next project. Remaining on the upward spiral.

"You can retire now," he said. "If you don't go back on the stage, no one will remember that moment of silence. No one will think you left because of the mistake."

"You don't need to lie to me," I said, not bothering to soften my voice. He wasn't going to manage me any longer and I wasn't going to listen to his directives. Childish, perhaps, but at that moment, small rebellions were all that I had left.

He plucked at the couch, his head down. His hair was thinning on the sides. He would need some reconstruction, and he didn't even realize it.

"All right then." He took a deep breath as if he were steeling himself against what he had to say. "The best thing you can do is retire. The Pané will remember, and so will the musical community. But they'll also remember that you had achieved top celebrity status once. For a little while, you were perfect."

The shaking was growing worse. I leaned against the desk just so that I could brace myself. I had to concentrate on my breathing, just like I used to do before a concert.

"You won't be able to get the best students," he said, "but you'll get the cream of the beginners. It'll be a good life. Not as glamorous as it had been before, but good."

Glamorous? He thought that performing in front of the Pané was glamorous? I remembered no glamour. Just concert halls and round eyes, watching, the hush as I walked onto the stages specially built for the new kind of music, the way my back ached after hours of holding myself rigid, and the headaches I had when I finished a successful concert.

Perhaps he enjoyed the meals, the hotels, the traveling, but I saw little of it. I couldn't mingle—the dry air in Pané restaurants made my throat tickle—and I rarely saw the outside of my suite, since the Pané didn't want to spend time with performers away from the concert halls.

"You still have a future," he was saying, understanding me well up until the last, "just not the one you were expecting."

He stood and met my gaze for the first time since he had come into the room. I finally saw him clearly, realizing that what I had always taken for intensity had been a reserve, an unwillingness to let his emotions get wrapped up in his business.

"I've done the best for you I could," he said, "although I don't expect you to understand that."

Then he nodded once and headed out of the study. I gripped the sides of the desk, my legs weak.

When he reached the door, he stopped. "And you might want to destroy all of that non-Pané music. It will only dilute your purity and should anyone find out you've been listening, corrupt your reputation. On other worlds, perhaps people still enjoy that stuff. But music on Pané has its own traditions, ones you were created especially for. Remember that."

Then he left, closing the door behind him.

I sank onto the overstuffed chair beside the desk. Created. He had said created. I thought I had been found.

I wondered what else I did not know about my own life.

I suspected it was a lot.

5

AFTER GIBSON LEFT with his new prodigy, I hid in the gardens and listened to every piece of music I could find—that is, every piece composed with humans, not Pané in mind.

I was stunned by the depth and breadth of it. The mixture of voices fascinated me—female sopranos and altos, and unaltered male tenors and basses.

I wasn't sure I liked the deep sound, but it entranced me nonetheless. Such freedom existed out there, away from Djapé, where this music was created.

Such freedom and so many opportunities.

It took me months, but I finally decided to make those opportunities my own.

6

I PLANNED MY ESCAPE from Djapé meticulously. I studied everything I could about travel routes off planet. Human settlements were more numerous than I realized, and I had hundreds of choices.

The problem wasn't where to go, but how to get there. Very few human transport ships ran between Djapé and other worlds. The performers couldn't travel to non-Pané approved worlds for fear of tainting their performances—or, more accurately, for fear of the perception of taint that would forever follow them from the trip.

Managers, handlers and merchants came and went with ease. But the successful managers and handlers hired their own transport. The merchants traveled on the cargo ships that supplied the small human colonies scattered across Djapé.

The supplies, I learned, were more numerous than I expected. Very little human food grew in Djapé's soil, and the Pané would not let humans disfigure the areas around their enclaves with greenhouses or hydroponic gardens. I learned that most of the food I had eaten throughout my life on Djapé had been imported, just as most of the material I wore and most of the furniture I sat on.

The Pané did not want humans to contaminate their world, even if they did want humans to perform for them. This so-called contamination included any kind of infrastructure. They allowed us our towns, but not industry or agriculture or even a real form of government.

Yet they expected us to police ourselves.

So much of what we needed on Djapé came from a space station called the Last Outpost. The Last Outpost was not the last human outpost in this sector, or in truth was in an outpost any longer. It was the only station between the nearest human-controlled world and Djapé, and it had become a community in and of itself.

Humans lived and worked on the Outpost. Entire generations had never left, tending to the ships, as well as to the diplomatic needs of the human community on Djapé.

Wherever humans lived and worked, they also needed entertainment.

All of my research confirmed that the best musicians in the sector rotated in and out of the Last Outpost. The Outpost had more bars, concert halls, and theaters than any other space station in this region—more, some said, than any other human-sponsored station.

The musically inclined (at least among the humans) actually vacationed at the Last Outpost to take in all the forms provided there. The Outpost itself was considered a music capitol by all three neighboring human worlds.

It even had its own conservatory, as well as a university with the best music department in the sector, and more informal instruction than any other city outside of the great and mythical Earth.

Gibson would not have approved, but Gibson no longer controlled me.

No one did.

And it was with that heady sense of freedom that I finally left Djapé, the place I had lived since I was three years old.

7

THE TRIP WAS NOT what I expected. The single transport that occasionally stopped on Djapé would not arrive for another two years. So I hired a cargo ship.

It was small and cramped, but the human crew left me to my own devices. We made the trip in thirty-six uneventful hours—a short time, it seemed to me, to make the transition from one life to another.

During the last few hours of the trip, I watched the Outpost appear in a portal. My research had told me the Outpost was unusual, but nothing had prepared me for the size of it. Interwoven rings, dozens, maybe a hundred, grew out of a small square station built centuries ago in this part of space. Each ring had a specialty and each ring had its own warren of buildings, living quarters and businesses.

For that reason, I hired a porter to meet me at the docks. He was a slight man with dark hair and a thin, petulant mouth. He brought a large cart with him, one that seemed to operate under its own power. When he saw that I had only two bags, he appeared surprised.

"Well, now," he said as I came down the cargo ship's passenger ramp, "this's the first time I've been called out for something I can carry in my own two hands."

My cheeks heated. I wanted to ask him if I had made some kind of social gaffe, but I did not. Gibson used to tell me that the only way others knew a man was uncomfortable was for him to admit it. *Performers*, Gibson said, *were never uncomfortable; nor did they make mistakes. They simply did things their very own way*.

I was already doing things my own way. My clothing marked me as different as well. On the cargo ship, no one wore robes, but I had nothing else. Here, too, in the docking area, I was the only person whose clothing flowed around his sandaled feet.

The porter took my bags and set them on his cart. They seemed somewhat forlorn there, as if they were waiting for a dozen other bags to join them. The porter helped me onto a seat at the front of the cart. He sat in the middle, pressing screen commands that were nearly invisible from my vantage.

We lurched forward, and I headed into my very first strictly human enclave. I sat stiffly, hands folded, as we left the nearly empty docking area, and emerged in the Last Outpost itself.

A cacophony greeted me. We went from clanging echoey near-silence to an amalgam of unrelated sounds. Voices carrying on dozens of conversations, children laughing, music blaring overhead. Our cart glided above the polished floor, but other carts had actual wheels that clack-clacked as they moved around us. People stood in front of open doors, hawking wares inside.

Shoppers merged with foot traffic and all the carts, talking, pointing, joking. Blue dresses jarred against orange pants which jarred against green hats. Brown coats, lavender shirts, white bandannas—no one wore the same uniform. No one wore the same colors.

The cart veered sharply to the left. Building facades lined the curved walls, each building a clear construct with a strict design code. Some were white with columns around the doors, others multi-colored, some with tiny round doors, others with irises that webbed open as something went by.

Those passing now were predominantly human, but some were not. One group of bipeds were covered in fuchsia-colored feathers. I couldn't tell if the feathers were a kind of clothing or part of their bodies. Others who passed had flippers instead of limbs, and still others waved their eyes on stalks, peering at me as if I were the exotic one.

"Short timers stay here," my porter said. "Those who come to the Outpost regularly have apartments in the permanent ring."

The permanent ring had an exotic sound to it. I tried to imagine living forever in this noisy, busy place, and found I could not. I had seen no windows since we docked.

Even if there were windows, they would only show darkness. I had always craved warmth and sunlight. I could not imagine being without them forever.

The cart glided into an archway. Dozens of other carts floated in the small space, all at varying height. The carts hummed, all at different frequencies, clashing and grating against my ears. The air here smelled slightly metallic, which meant that the gliders themselves gave off some kind of discharge.

The porter lowered his glider to a space in front of white double doors. The doors were carved with the name of the hotel in black flowing script.

I stepped gingerly off the glider onto a platform in front of the doors. Inside, lights as bright as the afternoon sun in my garden back home greeted me, soothing my jangled nerves.

I turned, about to grab the bags, when the porter grinned at me. "Door to door service," he said and lugged them inside.

I followed.

The lobby of this hotel—if one could call it a lobby— was cavernous. It felt like an outdoor spa. The bright lights hid the ceiling—above me it looked like a gigantic sun had obliterated the sky. Plants that I did not recognize, most of them green, grew out of the floor, grouping around the furniture, and adding a minty scent to the already perfumed air.

The tension left my shoulders and I felt, for the first time since I left Djapé, that I could relax.

The porter led me to a black marble podium, one I would not have seen without him. It was hidden by the leafy plants, which parted as we approached.

The porter set down my bags and extended a small silver disc. "Just a thumbprint," he said, "to verify it's you and your account will be charged."

I placed my thumb against the disc, which lit up. Then he nodded to me, pocketed the disc, and disappeared through the leaves.

I felt a slight pang at seeing him go. To assuage it, I turned to the podium. A lighted menu appeared above it. I checked myself in, then followed the written instructions. My bags were already moving on some kind of walkway toward my cabana.

I followed them.

My cabana resembled a small house. In fact, if I had not known I was on a station in space, I would have thought I was in some open but exotic domed colony somewhere.

The cabana had six rooms and two levels. Floor-to-ceiling windows covered the walls on the exterior side. The view constantly changed as the station slowly rotated.

I explored cautiously. The room that intrigued me the most was the dining area off the courtesy kitchen. A table sat on a clear floor, in a platform that extended out from the ring. When I sat on one of the chairs, I felt as if I were floating just outside of the station.

I finally understood how someone lived on the Outpost without feeling trapped or claustrophobic. I had known that the place was huge—one of the largest of its type anywhere in the sector—but I had thought that the darkness and the cramped quarters would make it feel like an underground cavern.

Instead, I felt like I was in a magical place, one that held the promise of a great future.

For the first time in months, I was at peace.

8

I MAPPED MY ASSAULT on the Outpost's musical venues as if I were planning a military campaign. In part, I knew that I would be an outsider, and I didn't want to call too much attention to myself. So my earliest visits would be at venues not too far from the guest ring.

But also, I didn't want to hear exceptionally exotic music. I was much more interested in music history, old Earth forms, truly human music with no alien influence whatsoever.

The first venue I chose was small and intimate, something called a blues club. The club itself was in a part of the Outpost called Saloon Central, a ring devoted mostly to clubs, bars, and restaurants that also dabbled in intoxicating substances.

I chose a table in the back away from the lights. A menu offered items I'd never heard of, from green chili to tamales to barbeque brisket—all, the menu claimed, authentic foods, but authentic to what I did not know. The air smelled tangy and sour, a scent that wasn't quite bad and wasn't quite good.

I ordered a beverage from a list I'd never heard of, something non-intoxicating called a C'cola, also considered "authentic" and a bowl of that day's special steak-and-potato soup.

Then I settled back and waited for the entertainment to begin.

The musicians did not file on stage as I had expected. Nor were they wearing matching clothing. In fact, they looked as though they were wearing their normal everyday dress. They carried instruments I had not seen before.

Slowly lights came up on the stage, revealing what I believed to be a percussion set—drums, was it called?—and some sort of keyboard instrument. I recognized two guitars and some kind of woodwind—a saxophone?—as well as a bass. Brass players—trumpeters?—sat near the percussionist in the back.

A rotund man sat on a stool in the center, one leg extended, the other supporting one of the guitars in the curve of its belly. The bass player sat on the right.

The remaining players sat near the side, holding their instruments down, all except the lone woman, who stood beside the rotund man in the center.

They crowded around their instruments, chatting so softly I couldn't hear them. Then the rotund man in the middle picked seven notes on his guitar.

They were almost a command to play music.

The others seemed to heed that command. The bass player plucked a long note. The keyboardist added a rolling chord, and the percussionist tapped one of the flatter instruments in the same rhythm the rotund man had played.

With the other hand, the percussionist played one-and-a-two-and-a-three, which then got picked up by the brass, almost as if they were answering the initial line.

It seemed disorganized. The music was loud. I could feel each instrument in my sternum, the bass line in particular so forceful that it seemed to propel my heart to a new rhythm.

Each time the rotund man played his signature line, he changed it. The changes made me uneasy, and once I caught myself looking to see how the Pané were reacting.

Only there weren't any Pané in the room.

Just humans of all sizes, most of them nodding their heads to the one-and-a-two beat carved (and kept) by the percussionist. Then the rotund man changed octaves, playing the same seven notes, only varying the motif, as if he were composing the song on the spot. When he reached the end of that variation, all the pieces came together: the original motif, the answer, and the percussion into one dramatic note, followed by a prolonged rest.

At that moment, the woman whirled toward the audience as if she suddenly realized we were there. She sang to us as if she were talking to us. Only she made the words fit that original motif. Her singing was low, in the same register as the rotund man's strings, and repeated in the same rhythm.

At the moment she hit the end of the sentence, the instruments joined her, just the same way they had joined the rotund man when he started the song.

She was swaying to the music. The entire ensemble swayed, as if they couldn't help themselves. I glanced at the audience. They were swaying too.

I was the only one who wasn't moving, and it took me a moment to realize the strain that was causing me. I literally had to hold myself in place, each muscle tense, so that I wouldn't move.

Movement caused the vocal chords to slip, the breath to fail, the wrong muscle to tighten at the wrong moment. If a performer moved, he ran the risk of making a fatal error.

Of course, in Tygher City, I had made a fatal error without moving anything except my lungs, my diaphragm, my throat, and my mouth. So even that theory, the theory of passivity, had been wrong.

Now the musical conversation had three parts: The woman, who sang her part as if she were making it up on the spot, the rotund man who continued his variations, and the rest of the musicians who either built a bed beneath her phrases or an answer to his.

I looked around again, afraid that someone would stop the music because of its myriad flaws, but no one did. Everyone was staring at the stage, bobbing their heads or tapping their fingers. Behind me, someone yelled, "Sing it, Sister!" and the woman didn't stop, she didn't chastise him, she didn't even seem to notice.

I turned and looked. The man at the door, the one who had taken my credits, didn't do anything, and neither did the servers.

Apparently, it was all right to yell in this place. Just like it was all right to move even when you were on stage.

They got to the end of her lyrics, following a similar, but not the same motif that the rotund man had set up with his strings. She created her own variations, and explored them with her voice, which grew louder and more raspy as the words became more fraught.

Finally, she told us she was done, and the music did as it had before: all the instruments came together in a single note, punctuated by a prolonged rest.

Then the other man—the one who had been talking with the woman—stepped forward and actually spoke to us, as if the rest of the musicians weren't there at all. What he was saying responded directly to her lyrics. He was answering her, like the musical phrases answered each other.

The complexity made my head hurt. The music had only gone on for a few minutes, but it felt as if time slowed down. Each phrase took on import, each beat seemed to reveal something new to me.

This wasn't music, not as I had heard music. This was something other, something visceral, something real.

The music came to that climactic pause again, and as it did, he and the woman turned to each other, mixing their lyrics together in a conversation—his words mimicking the background instruments' one-and-a-two rhythm, hers on that seven-note motif, so the entire opening of the piece, which had seemed so impromptu and random to me suddenly had purpose.

They had planned this, maybe even practiced each section, yet somehow retained a spontaneity that put me on edge, frightening me with its sheer audacity.

Only no one else seemed to think it audacious. They all seemed to expect this—the melody, the response, the not-quite-musical singing, the raspiness, and the increasing violence of the music, as the man and woman played at anger with each other.

I knew they were playing, yet as the music grew louder and louder, that anger seemed real. It was there in the strings, in the power of the keyboard, in the bass line, in the harder and harder rhythm of the percussion player.

I shifted my chair backwards, leaning against the wall, unable to go any farther. Never had music itself made me so uncomfortable—not the way it was performed, not the errors (of which there were dozens)—but the actual power of the notes, the force of the rhythm, the way that each sound built on every other sound creating so much emotional power that I became overwhelmed.

Finally, the song ended. The sound reverberated throughout the room, and slowly faded. I let out the breath I hadn't realized I was holding, my heart racing.

They started another song—this one with three hard beats from the percussionist, and then the entire group of musicians weighed in.

I couldn't handle more music. My heart already felt like it was going to explode. I'd felt more violent emotions in that six-minute song than I had felt in months—maybe since I saw Gibson with his new protégé. Or maybe even before that.

I pressed my thumb against the payment screen, then staggered out, stepping into the wide corridor. It seemed too bright after being in that club. People strolled past, some arm in arm, others having discussions. Tables filled with diners sat outside a few of the restaurants.

No one looked at me oddly. Apparently a man staggering out of the blues club wasn't unusual. I leaned against a nearby pillar and tried to catch my breath.

My heart wouldn't slow. My entire stomach churned.

I had had no idea that music had such intrinsic power. I had known that it was different, just from the recordings. But I had heard that difference in an intellectual way—with a fascination that different musical traditions could have such unbelievably different rules.

But I had never thought of music as an emotional pursuit—something that could control not only how I felt, but how I breathed.

Faintly, from inside the club, I could hear the wail of the rotund man's guitar, the rasp of the woman's voice. I stayed against the column, a safe distance away.

How had I missed this? I had devoted my life to music. And now it seemed as if I had only known a small part of it.

When I finally caught my breath, I wandered back to my cabana, and climbed inside that floating dining room.

I sat there without the lights on, staring at the blackness beyond—a blackness that wasn't entirely dark, because of the light from stars I couldn't identify. I sat in silence.

Only there was no silence.

Because inside my mind, I kept hearing that seven note motif.

Finally I tried it myself. It wasn't as easy as it sounded. My notes were pure and somehow wrong. I sang the line again, and heard how inappropriate my voice was. The woman's voice had been lower than mine. My voice was high, as high as the guitar on its fourth octave.

So I warbled the motif, like the guitar had done, and heard something in my own voice that hadn't been there before:

A wail. Almost a moan.

It caught me, and pleased me, and frightened me, all at the same time.

Ah, yes, the Pané had been right: other music corrupted. Other music changed.

I smiled softly to myself and sang the seven notes over and over again, each time making them different.

Each time, making them mine.

9

OF COURSE I WENT BACK: I couldn't help myself. Night after night, I listened to the same group of people playing different songs in different combinations of instruments.

At first, I couldn't stay very long. I sat rigidly and fled when the panic got too great. But slowly, I found myself relaxing. The toes of my right foot started tapping, only to stop when I noticed, or my head bobbed ever so slightly, just like everyone else's in the audience.

Gradually, over the space of a week, I managed to stay for seven songs. When they ended, the group left the stage, although their instruments remained. The audience remained as well, which I thought odd. The other patrons ordered more drinks, talked among themselves, even talked with the musicians—which shocked me. On Djapé, we musicians could not speak to the Pané. It was expressly forbidden unless the Pané spoke to us first.

I ordered another C'cola (those things were addicting) and watched the interactions. After about twenty minutes, the musicians meandered toward the stage, always led by the rotund man. When he sat on his stool, one knee supported his instrument—which I now knew as an electric guitar. The music dictionary I consulted called it "an outmoded instrument that uses an amplifier [which, in original instruments, used dangerous electric current] to make the vibrations of the strings louder or to alter them altogether).

I had looked up the blues as well. The definition told me why I had felt some unease. Central to the music was something called "blue notes," notes that fell somewhere between natural and flat on the third, fifth, and seventh degrees of a C Major scale. Those blue notes had the effect of holding the listener between the major and minor modes, without quite achieving either of them, providing either a sense of unease or, in most cases, a feeling of loss, of incompleteness.

The blues, then, was composed of half-flatted notes—abominations to the Pané.

Which made sitting in this venue, dim and claustrophobic, feel like rebellion to me.

It was as I had that thought that the musicians started up again, this time with an up-tempo piece. The singer—if he could be called that—was the rotund man. He had the most nasal voice I had ever heard. He seemed to sing from his throat instead of his diaphragm. And yet his vocals had power.

He sang three verses, then repeated the melody on his guitar, creating his own arpeggio in the middle of it all. The usual male singer had joined the trumpet player in the back, playing a smaller version of the same instrument, with a higher pitch and a brighter tone.

The various sounds these people could make with their instruments, the way that they answered each other and yet made everything seem casual amazed me. This time, this song, caught me, and I couldn't stop my toes from tapping or myself from swaying. I kept breathing too, which I hadn't in some of the earlier songs.

I relaxed into it, feeling, for the first time, like part of the audience. Before that, I had felt like an observer, an alien myself, someone who couldn't quite understand the experience everyone else was having.

I wasn't sure I still understood it, but I appreciated it—and with this song, I realized it had become part of me, so deep a part that I couldn't control my own physical response to it.

But I could finally move. I didn't have to be rigid any longer.

And that, more than anything, seemed like a victory to me.

10

AFTER THAT NIGHT, I managed to stay for the entire show. I got used to the cuisine, falling in love with the brisket and the steak-and-potato soup. I nodded to the doorman as I came in, and after a week, the waitress no longer had to give me a menu. Instead, she asked me which of my favorites I preferred, and brought me C'colas whenever my glass was empty.

The music had become an obsession for me. I'd been coming long enough to hear the musicians play some of the same songs over and over again. But startlingly, terrifyingly, they never played the songs in quite the same way.

The first time they changed a motif or played the electric guitar in place of the saxophone, I felt frightened. Had I, for the first time in my life, misremembered a piece of music? But later that same evening, as they played yet another song differently, I realized they had no set track. Unlike the music we performed for the Pané, there was more than one way to play these songs.

And that seemed like such a revelation to me that I finally felt I needed to consult with someone. Someone who knew what they were doing.

I wanted to talk to the rotund man.

11

I APPROACHED HIM after what he called a "set." He was always the first to climb onto the stage and the last to leave. After the first set of that evening's entertainment, he sat alone on his stool. He had unhooked his guitar from its strange amplifier, and he was plucking at the strings.

As I got closer, I could hear them, faint and precise.

He was tuning the guitar.

"Excuse me," I said. "May I ask you a question?"

He looked at me. Sweat beaded his forehead and lined the circles underneath his eyes. Up close, I saw that his shirt was drenched as well. It was hot on the stage. The heat from the small bar seemed to gather here. The amplifier, which I stood beside, seemed to give off some heat of its own.

"Sure," he said, his fingers flat against the strings on the guitar's neck. He no longer picked at it. "What do you need to know?"

I wasn't sure how to ask the question. I felt awkward and young, something I hadn't felt around music in a very, very long time.

"You never play songs in the same way," I said.

He waited.

"Isn't that—is that—isn't that...?" I didn't know how to finish the question. It kept getting jumbled in my mind between two separate thoughts: *Isn't that wrong? Is that disrespectful?*

Finally, instead of choosing between those thoughts, I blurted, "Doesn't music have rules here?"

"Rules," he repeated. He studied me for a moment. "Of course music has rules. It's all about rules."

"But you don't follow any of them," I said.

His eyes narrowed. He leaned back, his head tilting. It was as if he saw me for the very first time.

"Should you even be here?" he asked.

I flushed and lowered my head. I didn't want him to think I had deliberately stepped out of my place—whatever that place was.

"I don't know," I said. "If there are rules about who can be in this club, no one told me. If I'm supposed to leave—"

"No," he said. "That's not what I mean. You're one of those unfortunates, right? From Djapé?"

I raised my head. He was staring at me as if I were as alien to him as his music was to me.

"Unfortunates?" I repeated.

"One of those—what're you called?—castrati? Castrato? You...dress like one." He wasn't originally going to say dress. He was going to say "sound" or "speak." Others had said the same thing to me on the Outpost.

I had learned not to correct their ignorance, and to suffer their questions with as much grace as I could muster.

"I was raised on Djapé," I said cautiously.

"Which means you're one of their musicians, right? And from what I understand, they don't want you off the planet, let alone in a place like this, listening to us."

His words weren't harsh. They had a compassion and an interest that no one had shown me before.

"They no longer care what I do," I said.

"You got yourself fired?" His eyebrows went up. "I didn't know that was possible."

"No, I wasn't fired." My flush deepened. "I swallowed a note."

"You what?" He was leaning forward now. "What does that mean?"

"It means that I am no longer a trustworthy soloist, so my singing career is over." I spoke with a dispassion that surprised me. "I could have taught, but I chose instead to travel. I've never seen any place other than Djapé."

He frowned. "And you think this is where you should be?"

My heart was pounding as if his percussionist had gone back to work. "I've never heard music like this before. I had planned to go to other clubs, different venues. But I came here first. I've never heard anything like this. Not even on the old recordings. Your music is…evocative."

Words were so inadequate.

"And different," I said. "And technically, it shouldn't be. Technically, it's wrong."

"Wrong," he repeated.

My breath caught. Had I insulted him? I hadn't meant to.

"Each time you play," I said, "the songs are different. Are you making a statement by refusing to play the correct version of the song? Is it a rebellion?"

"The correct version of the song." He kept repeating my phrases as if we weren't speaking the same language, as if he had to hear the words in his own voice before he understood them. "What do you mean, the correct version of the song?"

"The composer's version," I said. "Surely, someone wrote it down or recorded it, showing how it should be played."

He blinked at me. "Don't you improvise on Djapé?"

"Improvise?" It was my turn to parrot him. I shook my head. "Humans lived under constraints on Djapé. Our lives were prescribed. We were not to deviate from any standard procedure. So, I suppose the answer is no, we did not improvise."

His eyes twinkled, as if my response amused him. "I meant musically," he said. "I was wondering if anyone taught you improvisation. But after what you just said, I doubt it now."

"Improvisation is a musical term?" I asked.

He nodded.

"You're making fun of me now," I said. "Music can't be improvised. It is all about precision and accuracy."

He rested an arm over the front of his guitar. "What would you have to be accurate about?"

"Following the composer's wishes," I said. "Making certain each note is hit precisely and held for the exact moment specified in the score."

"Seriously?" he asked.

"Yes," I said. "That's why I am asking you about your styles. Do the composers of your songs have more than one preferred text? Or are you making some kind of protest with your music? Is this an aspect of the blues that is accepted like half-flatted notes?"

"This—you mean improvisation?" he asked.

I shook my head. "Playing each song in a different manner than you played it the time before."

"We improvise," he said. "We let the music move us and we do what we feel when we feel it."

I couldn't wrap my brain around the concept. I was shaking my head as we spoke.

"Look," he said, "music follows rules. You were talking about them a minute ago. Haven't you taken theory?"

"I have sung," I said. "I haven't studied. There are theories to music?"

"Hundreds of them, just among humans alone, depending on the culture. We work out of a European Western tradition, based in ancient Earth texts. Blues evolved about a thousand years after the first known instances of repeated Western music. I would think you would be familiar with it. You're part of that tradition."

"I am?" I asked.

"Castrati," he said, "were extremely popular in opera—you know opera, right?"

I shook my head.

He raised his eyebrows. "I thought they were having you sing opera on Pané."

"No," I said. "We sing music specially written for and approved by the Pané."

"Man," he said, then grinned. "See? Even I have something to learn about music."

"You were saying something about opera and the musical tradition," I said.

"I was talking about castrati," he said. "They were really popular in the two hundred years before anyone ever thought of the blues. The castrati sang women's parts in Italian opera, but that probably doesn't mean anything to you since you don't know what opera is."

He shook his head in clear astonishment.

"Damn, I always thought you were following the operatic tradition. I thought you guys were singing the women's parts."

"Women do not sing for the Pané," I said. "It is forbidden. They are allowed to sing for humans in saloons, but only in the all-human areas."

"Weird," he said. "Fascinating, but weird."

Some of the other musicians had come back onto the stage.

"Look," he said. "I can't teach you anything about music or music theory or music history in a twenty-minute break. But we can continue the discussion at the conservatory tomorrow. I teach a three p.m. class in American folk songs, spirituals, and the blues. You could sit in if you want."

"I would like that," I said.

He extended his hand. I had seen this before on the Outpost. It was a sign of greeting and trust. I took his hand in mine. His skin was rough, as if it were made of a different substance than mine. His fingertips actually scraped my skin.

"I'm Jackson Scopes," he said. "Come find me tomorrow."

"I will," I said after I introduced myself. "And thank you."

I went back to my seat, thinking I wouldn't be able to concentrate on the music. But the rotund man—Jackson—started to play an eight-note combination on his electric guitar. Trumpets soared over it, added sixteenth notes and a glissando that sent shivers down my back. Then the percussionist joined in, and the woman started to sing.

I was lost, unease forgotten. The music swept me away, and I spent the rest of the evening in my chair, tapping my toes and reminding myself to breathe.

12

THE CONSERVATORY HAD ITS OWN RING. It was a smaller ring that encircled a section of the large higher education ring. Apparently, the conservatory had once been part of the higher education ring, like the two colleges and the university, but the conservatory became so famous and attracted so many students, that it needed additional space.

I hired a driver to take me to the conservatory, and I was glad that I did. As his two-person taxi glided through the corridors of the Outpost, he showed me the higher education ring, the conservatory, and the connectors on a glowing map that mostly covered one window. He was trying to give me instruction so that in the future, I could find the area myself, but all he managed to do was confuse me.

Still, I thanked him as he left me off in front of the American Wing of the Old Earth Campus on the Conservatory. Jackson's classroom wasn't far from the main doors. It was bigger than I expected, like a concert hall only with the stage at the bottom of the room, so that everyone looked down on the professor.

The students sat close to the front, so I remained in the back. Jackson stood in the very center of that lowered stage. Diagrams floated around him. All of them were music notations on a familiar five-line staff.

As Jackson touched each staff, music surrounded us. The notes on the staff moved as the music moved, showing us the notation that signified what the music was doing.

We were listening to a five-note melody, played in different lengths and different rhythms. Jackson got rid of the lyrics so that we could concentrate on the sound. The sound made me as uncomfortable as the blues had when I first heard it.

Even though the music seemed simple, with its variations on the same five notes, the sound produced was not. The song was something he called a spiritual, a father of the blues.

While I followed the moving notes, stunned at the variations rhythm could bring to the same piece of music, I didn't understand half of what he told us.

I didn't mind. I felt exhilarated as the class ended— not because of all I failed to understand, but because of what little I did.

Music had more depth and history than I had ever expected. What I had learned on Djapé was a small, narrow subset, one that had more to do with Pané tastes than human tastes.

As the class ended, I silently promised myself I would ask Jackson how I enrolled in the conservatory. I wanted to begin all over again, learn music anew.

The music ended, the notations disappeared, and slowly the students filed out. I remained in my seat. Jackson finished compiling his materials up front, placing the small discs in his pocket, and then climbed the stairs to me.

"What did you think?" he asked.

"I am stunned at all that I do not know," I said.

"And you want to learn, right?"

"Yes," I said.

He nodded. "Getting into the conservatory is hard—and expensive."

"Money is not a problem for me," I said.

"Finding space in a class, especially since you've already had a career, might be difficult. But I know who you can talk to."

He signaled me to get up.

"Come with me," he said. "I want to introduce you to the chief administrator of the Old Earth Wing."

"I assume from his title there are other wings?"

Jackson nodded as he led me out of the classroom. "The conservatory specializes in music from a variety of places. Mostly we focus on human forms, but there is a Pané wing, another wing for the Escarbemantes, and a few others. I don't listen to much alien music. I barely listen to human music of the post-colonial era. Mostly I listen to Old Earth forms."

As we passed door after door, I heard snatches of music. Some of it grand, with dozens of instruments, and some of it simple. A baritone sang arpeggios in one of the rooms.

We climbed four stairs to a floor that reminded me of my cabana. Floor-to-ceiling windows showed a truncated view. I could see the vistas of nearby space, but they were eclipsed by a walkway and a bit of the Higher Education Ring.

Couches covered the floor, with tables alongside. Scores floated by, tempting me to touch them so that I could hear the music they so clearly depicted.

"You can listen to anything you want," Jackson said, "so long as you use one of the private earcubes. We don't want you to disturb other passers-by."

The cubes sat on a nearby table. They were tiny, about an eighth the size of my smallest fingernail.

I looked longingly at them.

"Later," he said, "I'll get you permission to use one of the conservatory's music libraries."

"Thank you," I said. "You're being quite kind."

"Not really," he said. "You just intrigued me with your questions. I'm fascinated by the way you think."

He leaned into a door on the wall opposite the windows and called to someone named Felix.

A man came out of the door. He was tall, with a narrow nose and wide eyes. His lips narrowed when he saw me.

"This is the singer I told you about from Djapé," Jackson said. "He was quite well known—"

"You're early," Felix said to me as if I had done something wrong.

My face warmed. "I'm sorry. I didn't realize we had an appointment."

Jackson looked at Felix in confusion. Felix was frowning at me.

"I told your people we'd contact you when we were ready," Felix said. "We're not ready. We only have two. Normally we don't contact you until there are five or more."

"I'm sorry," I said again. "You must have me confused with someone else."

"You're from Djapé," Felix said. "You're here for the sopranos?"

My breath caught. "Boys?"

"What else?" he asked. "We should get another shipload in a month or so, and I'm told there are more on that."

"More sopranos?" I asked, my mouth dry.

Jackson was looking back and forth at us as if he didn't know what was going on. I didn't exactly either, but I had an inkling.

"We don't know if there are sopranos," Felix said. "But the incoming ship has an orphan wing. There are possibles. I thought you were going to wait until we could screen them."

Jackson took a step back from me. "I thought you didn't know anyone here."

"I don't," I said.

"Then what's this?" Jackson asked.

"I'm not sure." I folded my hands in front of my robe and leaned toward Felix. "You think I'm here to take boys back to Djapé?"

"Why else would you come?" Felix said.

I swallowed. "I came to the Outpost because of your music."

"I caught him listening to blues, Felix," Jackson said. "No true castrato from Pané would contaminate himself with human music."

"Then why is he here?" Felix asked.

I bowed, as I had been taught to do when I was most offended. I rose slowly, and said, "I am a windchime. I performed in the highest halls of Djapé, but my voice has failed me. I am a true castrato, as you say, but I am not here to bring others to Djapé. I am here to learn."

Felix blinked at me as if he couldn't quite believe what he was hearing. "Learn what?"

I folded my hands in front of my robe. "The forbidden music."

I said that last in a whisper. It was the first time I had admitted it to myself.

"You were offering him *kids*?" Jackson asked. "What the hell is that?"

Felix gave him a sideways glance. It looked furtive to me. "We have an agreement with the human musical colony on Djapé. If we encountered pure boy sopranos, we notify them. The Pané's tastes are so particular that they go through singers as if they were made of crystal. One bad shake and they've shattered."

The description was so accurate that I shuddered. It was one of the reasons we were called windchimes. A single crack, tiny and nearly invisible, could ruin a windchime's tone forever.

"You think it right to send a child into that mess?" Jackson asked.

"Why not? It's better than hiring them out to freighters at thirteen. That's what happens to most of the kids who come through here." Felix looked at me. "You lived a luxurious life, right? You have money. You're well off."

"I have money," I said.

"So you came for what?" Felix asked. "Reconstruction and reeducation?"

"Reconstruction is possible?" I asked.

"Sure," Felix said. "That's what most of the has-beens do when they get here. They get repaired and they go on to live normal lives."

"Without their voice," I said.

"Usually, they end up with a very musical voice," Felix said. "It is just a male voice. An adult male voice."

"Without the purity," I said.

"Humans rarely care about purity of tone," Felix said. "We outgrew that before we left Earth's solar system."

"It's Pané affectation," Jackson said, as if he were trying to convince me.

My breath caught. I thought of myself, singing those blue notes all those weeks ago, how odd my voice sounded. Yet how rich.

Both men were watching me. "You didn't come here for that either, did you?" Felix said.

I shook my head. "I came to see if I could enroll in the conservatory."

"Why?" Felix asked. "You already know Pané music."

"Jackson tells me there is an entire musical history I do not know. I would like to learn it."

Felix studied me for a moment. "You're not here for the boys?"

"No," I said. "Although I would like to meet them."

"Why?" Felix sounded wary.

"I am curious," I said.

"I can't believe this," Jackson said. "You sell children to the Pané?"

Felix straightened his back. "You know how the Children's Ring works. Don't sound so shocked."

"We don't usually sell children to aliens who'll disfigure them," Jackson said.

It was as if I was not in the room.

"We do not sell," Felix said.

"Maybe not outright," Jackson said, "but don't tell me there's no quid pro quo."

Felix shifted from foot to foot. "The Pané have generously agreed to fund the education of the other children. It's a small price to pay for the artistic richness we have given them."

"Artistic richness?" Jackson asked. "Those kids don't get a choice."

"It is what it is," Felix said. "They don't get a choice about being orphaned either."

I felt dizzy. I had no memories of my life before Djapé, although Gibson told me that I had come from another community and my parents were dead.

I am your family now, he had said to me in my earliest memory.

Only he wasn't family. He hadn't ever been family, only a man hoping to get rich off my talent.

"Have you always done it this way?" I asked Felix.

"I inherited the program," Felix said, with a glare at Jackson. "I wasn't sure I liked it at first either, but I toured the facilities on Djapé. Those kids live in luxury."

Jackson shook his head. He looked like he was about to speak.

"How long has this system been in place?" I asked.

"A century or more," Felix said. "I can look it up for you."

"So I came through here?"

Both men looked at me as if they suddenly realized that their discussion existed in more than theory.

"All human musicians get approved at the Outpost," Felix said.

"Just like the other merchandise." Jackson's face was red, but not with embarrassment.

With anger.

"I've heard no complaints," Felix said.

"That doesn't make it right," Jackson said.

"Ask your friend," Felix said. "Are you dissatisfied with your life?"

I did not know how to answer that question. My life was what it was. I couldn't imagine it any other way.

But then, I had little experience of other lives. What I knew about the universe, I had learned in the small human enclaves on Djapé.

"He's here, isn't he?" Jackson said. "Isn't that proof enough of dissatisfaction?"

"He's here because he did something to upset the Pané," Felix said.

"That's true," I said.

Jackson frowned. "Swallowing a note was enough to torpedo an entire career?"

"The Pané expect perfection," Felix said as if I weren't there. "That humans can achieve it, even for a short period of time, is nothing short of miraculous."

The warmth in my face increased. I didn't want to think about the Pané. But I did want to understand where I came from.

"Let me see the boys," I said.

"So you *are* here to take them back," Felix said.

"No," I said. "I had never thought of my life before Djapé. I would simply like to see what it had been like."

"Then you should see all of them," Jackson said.

Felix frowned. I thought he was going to say no, but he surprised me.

"Jackson is right," Felix said. "You should see all of them. Even the ones who aren't going to leave the Outpost."

My heart did a small flip, like it did when Jackson's musicians played a particularly interesting line of music.

"I would like that," I said. "I would like it very much."

13

THEY CALLED IT THE CHILDREN'S RING, but Felix told me that wasn't accurate. Not all children on the Outpost lived here, only the ones without family.

It was still a dangerous sector. People died all the time, leaving their children untended. Many children died, abandoned and alone.

Even more came to the Outpost, searching for some way to survive.

Eventually, the Outpost set up an area for them, complete with teachers and caretakers. If they were old enough, the children had to agree to live by the Outpost's rules—education and care in return for years of service wherever the Outpost deemed appropriate.

If the children weren't old enough to make a decision for themselves, they were offered for limited adoption. The limited adoption period lasted no more than two months. If no one took the children, they were then placed in the Children's Ring and expected to follow the same rules as all the others.

"Limited adoption?" I asked as we settled into one of the Conservatory's glide vehicles. Felix handled the controls. His position gave him all kinds of privileges within the Conservatory and parts of the Outpost. "What exactly does that mean?"

"The child doesn't have to become part of any family," Felix said. "But the person who sponsors the adoption guarantees the child's education and livelihood. Most of the children who go to Djapé do so under terms of a limited adoption."

"So I had one," I said.

"Most likely," Felix said. "This plan has been in place for decades."

I swallowed hard. My throat constricted. Still, I managed to ask, "Could I trace mine?"

"If you're still using the name you had when you arrived on the Outpost," Felix said. "And the only way to know that is to look."

Jackson sat in the back of the glide car. He wasn't watching either of us. Instead, he watched the door fronts pass us by. We had gone by several musical departments, all part of the Conservatory, and all of them leading into areas as large as the Old Earth Music Department.

The glide cart left the Conservatory through one of the bridges that led to the Higher Education Ring. We went through two other bridges between rings, each more crowded and cramped than the last, until we ended up in the Children's Ring.

It had straight walls and no apparent windows into the space beyond. The walls were decorated with multi-colored rectangles. It took me a while to realize that those rectangles were doors.

Felix glided the cart past schools, religious buildings, and storefronts, finally stopping at a wide building with double doors marked *Auditorium*.

"This is the induction center," he said. "Children spend their first week or so here, as they learn the rules, figure out where they fit, and get tested."

My shoulders were rigid. My hands, clasped over my stomach, were pressed so tightly together that my fingers ached.

"Tested for what?" I asked.

"Their various aptitudes," Felix said.

"To find out if they're musical," I said.

"Musical, mathematical, or have a facility for languages." Felix glided the cart into a pole that had locks along the edges. "As well as hundreds of other skills and talents."

"So they all have a place," I said, feeling more relieved than I expected.

"Of course not," Jackson said. "Some kids are too young to have skills. Others are too traumatized to even try."

He sounded bitter. He was clearly familiar with this place. I shifted on my seat so that I could see him.

"What happens to those children?" I asked.

"They're the ones who usually get shipped off by freighter at thirteen," Jackson said. "If they survive that long."

"Survive?" I asked. "Children die here?"

"It's not health," Jackson said. "It's cooperation. You have to work within the machine. If you don't, then you get moved."

"Moved where?" I asked.

"There is an area for troubled children," Felix said. He let himself out of the cart onto one of the glide platforms. He hit the button, sending himself down.

I felt disoriented. Felix hadn't wanted to discuss the troubled children. Jackson wasn't looking at me either.

"They die in the area for troubled children?" I asked.

Jackson shrugged one shoulder. "They don't thrive."

"How do you know this?" I asked.

He turned toward me. His expression was bleak. "You and I both came through this place. You received a limited adoption and lost body parts. I was trouble. I worked a freighter."

"But you have a teaching position now," I said. "You play music every night."

"Where do you think I learned about the blues?"

"They play blues on freighters?" I asked.

Jackson smiled faintly, almost contemptuously, and shook his head. "Did you like living on Djapé?"

My garden rose in my mind. And the music, playing softly in my study. The forbidden music. The way my back tensed before I went on stage. The feeling of relief and terror that happened as my voice cracked.

"I don't know," I said.

"I hated the freighter," he said. "I hated what Felix calls the Trouble Area. You didn't hate Djapé."

"Hate is a strong word," I said.

"And I've noticed that you don't use strong words." Jackson shrugged. "Go visit. See what you think."

My heart was pounding.

"How do I get down?" I asked.

"Touch the pole," Jackson said. "Your glide platform will appear next to the door."

I had to lean forward to touch the pole. It vibrated slightly under my fingertips. Within seconds, the platform appeared beside the car, a square bit of flooring that looked unstable to me. Still, I let myself out, balancing myself with my hands on the pole and the glide car.

"Are you coming?" I asked Jackson.

His face was gray. He looked vaguely ill. "No."

I studied him for a moment, but he didn't meet my gaze any longer. Instead, he looked at the neighborhood as if he had never seen it before.

I left him. The platform took me down slowly. It felt rickety, as if I moved wrong, I would fall.

I held myself rigid. The platform landed, and I staggered slightly to the left.

Felix was waiting beside the double doors.

"Did Jackson try to talk you out of coming?" he asked.

"No," I said. "But he's not going to join us."

Felix gave me a sideways, somewhat distracted grin. "You know he grew up here."

"He told me," I said. "I didn't expect it."

"You should have. I think a good fifty percent of the permanent workforce came through the Children's Ring."

He pulled the doors open, stepping inside. The interior was dark compared with the main thoroughfare we'd traveled along.

"Did you?" I asked as I followed him into the dimness.

"No," he said. "I'm one of the lucky ones. I was hired for my expertise."

"With children?" I asked.

This time he did look at me in surprise. "In Ancient Music, particularly Earth forms."

"I'm surprised the Outpost found that a valuable skill."

"It wasn't the Outpost," he said. "It was the Conservatory. They needed someone with a broad range of knowledge to handle the Old Earth Department. All human music was born on Earth. Those forms are the most important."

"All human music," I said slowly. "Even what we sang on Djapé?"

"Especially what you sang there," he said. "The diatonic scale—the eight whole notes—comes from Ancient Greece. The hexachords that you also sang were developed in Europe in what was called the Middle Ages, and arpeggios, especially those sung in descending order, which were first developed in a period called the Renaissance."

"But I was told that the Pané had unique musical tastes," I said.

"Most humans do not listen to pure notes or broken chords and consider them entertainment. To humans, they are part of a great whole, a symphony or a song. To the Pané, they are the entire performance."

We had gone deep into the building. It had no windows. Only doorways marked with numbers running alongside the hallway. Eventually the hallway opened up, revealing another set of double doors.

"I contacted the headmistress here," he said. "The boys are waiting for you."

He made it sound like I was still going to choose them. My stomach clenched.

"They don't think I'm going to adopt them or anything, do they?" I asked.

He shook his head. "They only know that you want an audition. That is what you want, isn't it?"

I wasn't sure what I wanted. "Is that what you do when someone comes from Djapé?"

"Scales and arpeggios only," he said. "Would you like to hear that?"

It was what I understood. But I didn't want to set up the wrong expectations.

"Whatever they have prepared is fine," I said.

He made a small grunt, as if I had disappointed him, and then we stepped through the doors.

I had expected an auditorium—something with a stage and chairs. While this room was large, it was nothing more than an empty space. The floor did slope downwards slightly, but that seemed to be more of a design flaw than anything else.

A woman stood to one side and when she saw us, she waved a hand. A group of boys filed in. They ranged in age from about ten to four or five. At the end of the group, four women brought in very little children. The women held their hands as the boys half-walked, half-tumbled forward. Some were so young that they hadn't mastered walking very well yet. Others had obviously been raised in zero-g and weren't used to walking in gravity.

"Only boys?" I asked.

Felix gave me a withering look. "No other aliens care about our music. And the Pané only want male sopranos."

I almost protested again that I was not here for the Pané, but I did not. He had thought I was interested only in the children that might go to Djapé—and maybe I was.

"We'll start with the little ones," Felix said. "Let's just go one by one."

Each little boy paraded forward. At the urging of the woman who had led him in, he would sing a diatonic scale. All of the little ones had beautiful voices, but only one sang with such purity that my hair stood on end.

He was tiny, with big brown eyes and hair cut so short that it stood straight up on top. He didn't seem to understand why anyone wanted him to sing, but all the woman had to do was name the note and he sang it with clarity and such accuracy that if I tested the note mechanically, I would have found him to hit the center of the pitch—no variation, not even a fraction of a fraction off.

"He's one of the two, isn't he?" I softly asked Felix. Felix nodded.

I walked up to the boy and crouched.

"Sing after me," I said, and proceeded to sing the C Major arpeggio that I had destroyed in Tygher City.

The boy sang with me—C-E-G-C-G-E-C—his notes so pure and fresh that shivers ran down my spine.

He didn't know what he was singing. He was just making sounds. Lovely sounds, but nothing more.

The older boys watched, rapt. The youngest boys squirmed, held fast by the women who had brought them in. Everyone was staring at me.

"Thank you," I said to the little one who sang for me.

He gave me a wide grin, and then ran back to his handler. He hugged her thigh.

I frowned as I saw that. He had made a connection here, whether he had known it or not. He would not be able to hug a woman like that on Djapé. Not without special permission.

Then I stood, and backed up.

"Let's hear the rest of you," I said.

The woman who had called them all in clapped her hands together. They looked toward her. Then she waved her hands in a fashion that seemed to give them direction.

One quarter of them started. They sang in perfect unison, singing the entire verse. Then they started over, and when they got to the end of the first line, another quarter of the group started at the beginning. When the second group got to the end of the first line, the third quarter chimed in. And when they reached their line, the final quarter joined.

I had never heard the song sung this way—and it became instantly clear that the song had been designed to be sung like this. The harmonies were lovely, the boys' voices strong.

And like a perfect chorus, no voice stuck out.

One of the oldest boys on the side closest to me sang with such complete joy that my eye went to him immediately. He smiled as the harmonies grew more intense and his body swayed as if he were listening to one of Jackson's performances in the blues' club.

The boys finished and the chords echoed through the auditorium. Now I knew how the place had gotten its name. Its acoustics were perfect.

"Let's hear it again," I said, "but this time, with only one person from each group."

I didn't care who the first three were, but I wanted to hear that joyful boy. So I picked three others from the sections and him. He had been in the final group, so he would have a solo at the end, but he wouldn't start.

The boy who started wobbled his way through the opening line. He was clearly terrified, his throat closing and constricting the notes. He didn't lose pitch, but his tone was muddy.

The second child joined, then the third. The fourth—the boy I was interested in—tilted his head back and opened his mouth, blending perfectly. Again he sang with joy.

As each part dropped out, his became stronger. At the end, he sounded like the entire chorus all by himself.

And like that little boy who sang for me, this boy had a purity of tone that sent shivers down my spine.

"You're amazing," Felix said to me. "You found the other one."

It wasn't hard. I had grown up listening to voices like that. But I nodded.

"Thank you," I said to the boys. "Thank you all."

I thanked the women as well, and they nodded at me. Then the one who had directed the chorus asked Felix if they could leave. He looked at me.

I nodded, and the boys filed out.

"Satisfied?" he asked.

But I wasn't. I felt even more uncomfortable than I expected—not because this performance raised memories. It didn't. But because of the children themselves.

I must have been as young as that first boy when I left the Outpost. I had no memory of a time before Djapé, and I had vague memories of imitation singing, much like I had the boy do for me. It was the way the youngest children learned to sing in the Pané style.

But the older boy bothered me. He had already learned music—this culture's music—and he loved it.

"You can't send that older child to Djapé," I said to Felix. "The Pané will destroy him."

Felix frowned at me. "You can't know that."

"I know it better than you," I said. "They'll teach perfection, not enjoyment. Each note is an exam, not a linked unit with any other note. He may spend years there, but he'll never be a top-level performer, and he will learn to hate his gift."

Felix glanced toward the door the boys had left from.

"So that's why you wanted to come," he said. "To prevent children from going to Djapé. I told you how entrenched this system is, how the Pané money helps the other children—"

"Yes," I said. "You told me, and I believe you. The youngest one is exactly what they want. He is a mimic. He makes sounds, pure sounds, not music. He is a human windchime, and they will love him."

Felix was still watching me warily. "I still hear hesitation in your voice."

I sighed. I was guessing at this last part. "He has affection for the woman who brought him here. You shouldn't break that up."

"Women can't contaminate the performers," Felix said.

"You could argue that she's already had an influence, and it can't be heard in his voice. Make her a deal-breaker."

He stared at me. "You guarantee that the Pané will like him?"

"Yes," I said. "I spent my entire life in that system. I know what they're looking for."

"You realize his happiness isn't an issue," Felix said.

"It seems that happiness isn't an issue for anyone here," I said, not telling him that I never thought of happiness either. "But if he has someone to care for him, he'll perform better, and maybe he'll survive longer than some of the others who come to Djapé."

Maybe he wouldn't have a horrible realization, like I had, that the person he thought cared about him only cared about his perfect voice.

"Why would he survive longer?" Felix asked.

"Fear," I said. "Voices shatter from the sheer terror of making a mistake. I was raised to be perfect or I would be rejected. Maybe if he has someone who cares for him as him, he will not be afraid of such rejection. His voice won't constrict. He'll perform from strength, not from terror."

Felix continued to stare at me, and then he shook his head. He grinned, just a little. "You want my job?"

"I know nothing about Old Earth," I said.

"Picking voices for the Pané," he said.

"No," I said before I could edit my response. "I want to study every form of music possible. I want to break the habits I learned on Djapé, not embrace them."

"So you're a lot more like that older kid. You love music," Felix said.

I thought of those stolen moments in my study, the revelations in the blues club, the odd sound to my own voice as I tried that seven-note opening.

"I was nothing like that boy," I said. "I was a windchime, just like the little one. But I stumbled on some recordings, and they changed me."

The recordings had frightened me too, but I wasn't going to tell Felix that. They had frightened me because they had contaminated me, and I had let it happen.

I might even have let that vocal break happen, just to escape the repetition of performance, the nightly striving for perfection.

"If you sent the older boy to Djapé, you would change him in the wrong way. The younger one, he would have the good life you told Jackson about. And if the younger boy chooses something different when he gets older, then so be it. But you would be forcing the older child into a mold that doesn't suit him."

"One child, not two," Felix said, almost to himself. "They're not going to like this."

"One child who sings longer. One child who loves what he does. Usually you send two because one will break, right?"

He looked at me. His gaze was measuring. It was as if I had uncovered a secret even he didn't want to acknowledge.

"It's always been that way," he said. "You send two, one breaks. And no one has been able to predict the break."

"Because you have to know what life on Djapé is like, and you don't know that," I said.

"But you do."

Too well.

"Don't send the one who'll break," I said. "Send the woman instead."

"They hated women's voices," he said as if I didn't know.

"She's not going there to sing," I said. "She's going to make sure he does."

"By taking care of him," Felix said. He turned away from me, but not before I saw the relief on his face.

"Yes," I said.

"Are you telling me no one takes care of these children?"

"No, I'm not saying that." I looked at the door where the children had filed out. I had no idea what level of care they received here. I supposed I could ask Jackson.

"Then why send the woman?" Felix asked.

"The children get good care," I said, "but they—we—are commodities. And if we break, no one puts us back together."

"Is that what happened to you?" Felix asked.

"As an adult," I said. "But I know it happens to the young ones. I've seen it."

"What happens to them then?" Felix asked.

I frowned. I didn't exactly know. The ones I had seen got led off-stage, never to perform again.

"They grow up to become support staff, I think," I said. "I don't exactly know."

Sadly, ironically, I had never thought about it before.

Felix walked to the front of the room. He was clearly thinking about what I said. He clasped his hands behind his back, paced as if he were retracing the boys' steps, and then walked back to me.

He nodded. "I can make this work. I know I can."

His mood seemed suddenly lighter. I let out a small breath of air I hadn't realized I had been holding.

Maybe this all disturbed me more than I wanted to admit. Such a big system, and these boys were only a small part of it. The entire Outpost had developed around the orphans. And if they had been farmed out throughout the decades, then they had an impact throughout the entire sector.

But Felix clearly wasn't thinking of that. He was thinking of our discussion. He clapped a hand on my back and led me out of the auditorium. As we walked down the hall, he said: "If I do this, you'll have to agree to listen to the future candidates."

It wasn't a question. It was a command. I bristled at commands.

"I already said I don't want your job," I said.

"I'm asking you to consult," he said. "In exchange for the right to study at the Conservatory."

I wanted to say no, but that might have been a reaction to his preemptory statement. I also wanted to study at the Conservatory. I wanted to study human musical traditions. I wanted to learn everything I could about the art I had just so recently discovered.

I could do some of that simply by attending the bars, clubs, and concert halls on the Outpost. But the last week of listening to Jackson's performances had raised questions too complicated to answer in a single night's performance.

Still, I wanted to make my own decision—and not one based on Djapé or the Pané or sending boys to a life just like mine had been.

"I want to think about it," I said.

My silence must have told Felix about my ambivalence. He nodded.

"Fair enough," he said.

14

I SPENT THE NEXT THREE DAYS thinking about Felix's offer. Only I wasn't thinking so much about the trade as I was about myself. I had never done a lot of self analysis. I was just stumbling onto it here, and it felt as uncomfortable as the music I first heard in the blues club.

Windchimes did not feel emotion. Windchimes simply let air pass through their instrument, achieving a purity of sound that was in their very nature. Not because they had brought the emotion to the surface. Not because they had felt anything, except maybe a cold breeze.

The fear came because the instrument could become flawed. The chimes could crack, the wind could shatter a delicate part of the glass itself. And then nothing, not even the most careful repair, could remake the sound.

Sound was notoriously fickle. Its perfection was short-lived.

Perhaps that was why blues had intrigued me so much. The blues did not seem to recognize perfection.

The blues seemed to spurn it.

The older boy had felt emotion when he sang. The younger boy had not. He hadn't even thought of music as anything other than sounds that traveled through his instrument, through his voice.

Perfection could be trained. It could be achieved by a blessed few. I had done so. That child might be able to as well.

Oddly, at least to me, I felt less conflicted about choosing the children than I did about my own motivation for doing so. When I left Djapé, I hoped to leave permanently. I had kept my home there, yes, because I was afraid (that word again!) that I would not survive the universe outside of the one I had known.

But I could survive here, even if I did not join the Conservatory. I could spend the rest of my life here, listening to music, discovering new theories, and learning to use my voice in a new way.

I did not go to the blues club during those three days, but I did go back to the Children's Ring. I asked for—and received—my records.

Apparently Gibson, who had taken me from the Outpost, had kept my name.

I had been three, just like he said. One of ten survivors of a mid-space collision between a passenger ship and some kind of space debris. The pilots survived. A few of the crew had taken the children first to a secure area. By the time they were ready to take the parents, they realized that the back section of the ship had opened to the coldness of space.

All of the children had been brought to the Outpost, where the authorities had followed standard protocol: they had searched for the remaining family. Some of the children had grandparents and aunts and uncles. I had had no one, except the two people traveling with me. People who were listed only by their names, and the fact that they were traveling to the Outpost to look for work.

"Charity cases," the woman who helped me with the records said. "Sometimes the Outpost does that. It funds a ship of job seekers. It's hard to get good workers out here, and even harder to keep them."

"So I would have ended up on the Outpost no matter what," I said.

She nodded. "And probably not have been tested for music. You would have lived with your parents and most likely had minimal education. You would have ended up as they had."

"Dead?" I asked.

She laughed. "No," she said. "Whatever jobs they found themselves in were the jobs you would have been considered for."

"Work is hereditary here?" I asked.

She shook her head. "But families tend to follow the same paths. The new jobs are filled by the children from the Ring—the talented children of the Ring, of course."

Her comments sounded self-serving to me, so I investigated them, and found, indeed, that employment studies of the Outpost had shown the most driven employees were not members of the families who lived here, but the children who had been orphaned. They had learned competition, the value of hard work, and how to maximize their own skill set.

Which was what I was now trying to do. I had a beautiful voice—albeit unconventional for the Outpost—and a growing love of all types of music. A curiosity that had gotten me in trouble on Djapé and might serve me well here.

A curiosity that seemed to grow the more I learned.

After the three days, I returned to Felix and accepted his offer. I would help him choose the right children for Djapé and he would guarantee me a permanent place of study in the Conservatory.

But I did have one condition. If I felt a perfectly pure boy soprano would be destroyed on Djapé—and there were no others to take his place—the Pané and their human minions would be told that there were no boys in that group. Fewer children would go to Djapé, but those who would might actually have a chance at long-term musical (and personal) survival.

Felix agreed. He offered to take me to dinner to celebrate, but I refused.

Instead, I went to the blues club.

Jackson's band was at the end of a song. Instead of fading out as he usually did, Jackson started a completely different song. The band members looked at him, and then the percussionist grinned. He caught the syncopated beat. So did the bass player. The saxophonist did his own riff. The female singer grabbed a tambourine off the percussionist's table and tapped it against her hip on the off-beats.

I made my way to my usual table. The waitress was already setting down my C'cola when Jackson started singing, *Playin' With My Friends*. I had heard it before, but never so energetically.

He was looking at me as he played, inviting me through the lyrics of the song, to join them on stage. He even beckoned as he sang that I could pick any song I wanted to, so long as it was the blues.

I shook my head and sat down. He grinned at me, and stopped singing, playing a variation on the melody that I had never heard before. The entire band played without a singer for another fifteen minutes, various versions of the same song, with each instrument taking the melody—except the percussionist, who kept the same syncopated beat to the entire piece.

It was one of the most interesting—and welcoming—songs I had ever heard them do. By the end of it, I was clapping with the tambourine's beat like everyone else.

Finally Jackson eased out of the piece, followed by the bass. The percussion, tambourine and trumpets finished it off with a flourish. Then everyone bowed, and threaded off the stage.

Jackson leaned his electric guitar against his stool. He climbed down into the audience as well, and startled me by coming to my table just as the steak-and-potato soup did. He ordered his own C'cola and a side of brisket.

"Why didn't you come up?" he asked. "I know you can sing."

"Not like that," I said. "Try as I might, I can't achieve a half-flatted note."

"Achieve it?" He raised his eyebrows. "You don't achieve notes. You sing them."

I shrugged. "I can't sing them either."

"Lemme hear you," he said. "Come on up to the stage."

I shook my head. "You have an audience."

"So?" He finished his C'cola as he stood, then set the glass on the table. "Come on."

"The last time I sang for anyone," I said, "I swallowed a note."

He laughed. "Hell, we're lucky if we even hit them."

That was true. I exhaled, and I stood reluctantly. My stomach had clenched, but to my surprise, my throat hadn't.

I climbed onto the stage and stood with my back to the small crowd. "What do you want me to try?"

"Something Pané," he said. "Something you're used to."

"No one here will like it," I said.

He nodded. "I want to hear it."

So I sang part of Tampini's Aria in E Major. I hit each note perfectly. They sounded too large in the club, ironic, I thought, considering the power of the blues band before me.

Jackson was grinning. "That's Pané music, huh?"

I nodded. "It's certainly not blues," I said.

"So sing for me," he said. "This line."

He sang the opening lines of the song that the band had just done. I sang as softly as I could, knowing how embarrassingly strange my pure high voice sounded.

"Keep going," he said, as I faded out. "You know the words."

And I did. Music stayed in my head. So I sang the opening lines of *Playin' With My Friends*, and he built a bridge underneath me with the electric guitar. Shivers were running down my spine.

I had always thought I was a windchime, but Jackson's song was making me into something else. As I sang, the other band members filed back on stage. They picked up in the middle as if they had never quit, only I was singing the melody. Jackson kept the bridge beneath me, and I kept my back to the audience. We played through all three verses and two renditions of the chorus, and then Jackson nodded at me to stop.

The band played twelve more bars and stopped as well. There was a moment of silence—the Pané version of a boo—and then someone clapped. Others followed. The applause was so steady and fierce that it threatened to overwhelm me.

I hadn't moved. Jackson had to set down his guitar and grab me by the shoulders, turning me around. The audience was on its feet, clapping and stomping and asking for more.

"But it's not the blues," I said to Jackson.

"Not the old-fashioned kind, that's true," he said. "This is something new. That's what they're applauding. Something different."

"Is that good?" I asked.

He extended a hand to the still applauding crowd. "What do you think?"

I thought I had never experienced a reaction that so moved me. The Pané's pleasure allowed me to keep my job. Here I had no job. I had experimented—and it had succeeded.

"Join us for another song?" he asked.

I started to shake my head, then changed my mind.

"Just one," I said, "and no more."

Five songs later, winded and covered in sweat, I staggered off the stage. The waitress brought me a fresh bowl of soup, some water, and another C'cola. The audience congratulated me and asked me when I was going to sing again.

Jackson grinned. "He'll be back," he kept promising.

"I can't," I said to him as he sat back down at my table. "I don't sing like you do. There's no music like this."

"Precisely," he said. "That's what's so wonderful about it."

"It doesn't follow any rules," I said.

"So there can't be perfection," he said.

I stared at him for a moment, stunned at what he just said. No perfection? Not even a little?

"We'll start slowly," he said. "One night a week. We'll put a sign out front, and call it the Pané Blues."

"Isn't that a contradiction?" I asked.

"Music loves dissonance," he said. "You just haven't learned that yet."

He was right. I hadn't learned dissonance. But I had a hunch I would.

And if my previous experiences on the Outpost were any example, I might actually come to love it.

"One night," I said, "and no more."

He grinned. He knew, as well as I did, that my vows that night weren't holding up.

I wasn't sure I wanted them to.

I was acting without thinking, just like I had done in that concert in Tygher City, when my voice broke. My perfection broke. My life broke.

And became something new.

Something flawed.

Something better.

ABOUT THE AUTHOR

INTERNATIONAL BESTSELLING WRITER Kristine Kathryn Rusch has won two Hugo awards, a World Fantasy Award, and six *Asimov's* Readers Choice Awards. Her latest science fiction novels are *Blowback: A Retrieval Artist Novel, Snipers,* and *Skirmishes,* the next novel in her Diving Universe series. She also writes mysteries under the name Kris Nelscott.

For more information about her work, please go to kristinekathrynrusch.com.

Also by
Kristine Kathryn Rusch

FICTION RIVER: YEAR ONE